This book belongs to

_____

_____

Angel, angel watching over me, take my bad dreams away from me.

1

Now it's time to rest your head,
so the fairies and angels can sit on
your bed.

Butterflies and rainbows will be in your dreams, because fairies and angels love you and give you sweet dreams.

4

I have a dream catcher my angel gave to me. To stop my bad dreams chasing after me.

I hang it above me when I go to bed, and the dream catcher catches it in its shiny web!

Come here angel, come and see!
Look at fairy, she's watching over me.

At night when I'm sleeping she sprinkles magic dust. To take away my bad dreams, it really does.

She giggles and smiles, I see her through squinted eyes. Then she blows me a little kiss and says goodnight.

Last night I woke up from a scary dream. I yelled and shouted but no one was to be seen. Then suddenly a bright light shone, and a feather was floating down.

I heard a gentle whisper "It's me your angel sweetheart, please lay your head back down. No need to be afraid as I am with you now."

Sprinkle me with fairy dust
watch and see...

All my bad dreams
drift away from me!

Bad dreams, bad dreams disappear.
Good dreams, good dreams will you
appear.

There will be candy canes, candy floss and fairies too. You'll have good dreams because the angels are watching over you.

Peeking through the curtains I see two eyes looking at me. Could it be my angel? YES! She's waving at me.

"Hello little one, would you like a hug? I will tuck you in to make you snug as a bug."

Look! There's a fairy with a bag of
magic dust. "Sprinkle it!" said angel,
sprinkle lots of dust!

"Of course, I will" said fairy. But first little one, close your eyes up tight and we will sing you a bedtime lullaby.

Goodnight, goodnight my little honeybee.

You are, you are, so precious you are to me.

Goodnight, goodnight my little honeybee.

You are, you are, so precious you are to me.

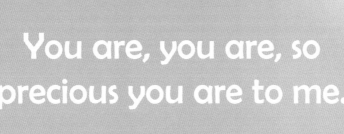

# Here you can draw your dreams...

Sweet dreams and
goodnight.

Printed in Great Britain
by Amazon